For Mum and Dad, Dave, and Conrad - JH

For Mum, Gran, and David (the original Davy Dark) - KW

First edition for the United States, its territories
and dependencies, and Canada published in 2006
by Barron's Educational Series, Inc.

Text © Jim Helmore 2005
Illustrations © Karen Wall 2005

This version of *Letterbox Lil* is published by
arrangement with Oxford University Press.

All inquiries should be addressed to:
Barron's Educational Series, Inc.
250 Wireless Blvd.
Hauppauge, NY 11788
www.barronseduc.com

ISBN-13: 978-0-7641-5893-3
ISBN-10: 0-7641-5893-7

Library of Congress Catalog Card No.: 2004118232

Printed in China

9 8 7 6 5 4 3 2 1

Letterbox Lil

-a cautionary tale-

Jim Helmore & Karen Wall

BARRON'S

This is the story of
Letterbox Lil.

On the street where she lived
there is talk of her still.

By
day
or by night
from her house
she would
sneak.

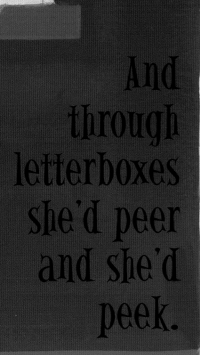

And through letterboxes she'd peer and she'd peek.

If you dare to read on,

I promise to tell

of the things that Lil saw –

they may make you unwell .....

At number seven,
alert and awake,
there sits adorable
Tiffany Take.

But she has
been left with
her brother's
pet snake!

Do children taste better

than chocolate cake?

Davy Dark
lives three
houses down,

in bright sunlight
he wears a frown.

By night
he's the happiest
boy in town...

with two
pointed teeth
and a
vampire's
gown!

And next door
to Davy,
Professor Plotz

is getting
some help from
his friendly
robots...

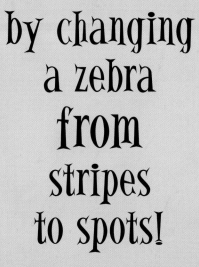

by changing
a zebra
from
stripes
to spots!

I hope he
won't mind
all those
polka dots!

Then Letterbox Lil
spied on
Long-Legged
Peter.

His looks
and his clothes
could not
have been neater.

But don't be misled:
he's a sly
spider-eater!

His tongue
at full

stretch

measures
more than
a meter!

Lil wasn't put off
by the horrors she saw.
Spying was fun,
so she peeped more and more.

Dragons and witches
in books were a bore
when compared to what
lay behind any closed door!

Then one day
Lil opened
her last letterbox.

LETTERS

From the hairs
on her head...

to the toes
in her socks,

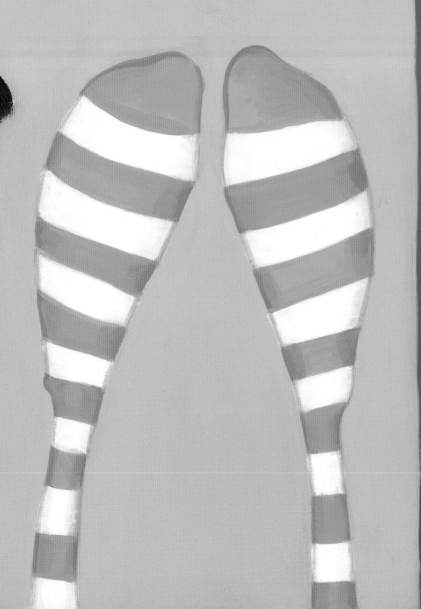

she was shaken
with shock,

she was frozen
with fear.

Since then, letterboxes
she'll never go near .....

And what she saw,
it frightens her still...

So from that shocking day to this,
peeping is something that Lil doesn't miss.

Spying is fun, it's undoubtedly true,
but not when the person
that's spied on
is you!

And this, my friends,
concludes the tale.
Good night,
sleep tight,
don't look so pale.....

"But don't finish there!" I hear you all shout.
"What looked back at Lil? We want to find out!"

A monster that roars
with slobbering jaws?

A beast from the deep
coiled up in a heap?

Or something that's loud and incredibly **smelly**, with ears on its chin and a nose in its belly?

Come close and I'll tell in the softest of whispers...

those bright eyes belonged
to sleek Willow Whiskers!